# The King's Castles

# The King's Castles

Kitty Anthony

*Illustrated by Bonnie Heppe Runge*

THE BANNER OF TRUTH TRUST

THE BANNER OF TRUTH TRUST
*3 Murrayfield Road, Edinburgh EH12 6EL*
*PO Box 621, Carlisle, Pennsylvania 17013, USA*

First published 2000
ISBN 0 85151 777 3

Typeset in 12/16pt Palatino
at the Banner of Truth Trust, Edinburgh
Printed and bound in Great Britain by
Cromwell Press, Trowbridge, Wiltshire

# Contents

# he Castle Keep

NOW THIS IS A STORY about Lily and Norman, two people who may seem like some girl and boy you know. Lily was short and round, with fat brick-red curls and enough freckles on her nose to win a contest – which she did at least once. Also, she talked a lot for an eight-year-old person. Norman was quiet and thin, and three years older than Lily.

Oh, yes! He was the *older brother*! Sometimes Lily thought an older brother was nice to have around. He had sandy blond hair which flew up in the air with the slightest breeze, and there was even one little clump that always stood straight up on the top of his head and refused to lie down neatly. Because Norman wore round eyeglasses, he usually looked older than his eleven years. Unfortunately, there were times when Norman could be a trial.

'Stay out of my room, Lily!'

'But, Normy—'

'And don't call me Normy!'

Lily could have forgiven Norman almost anything, but there was that time in the hall on the third floor of their big city house when Norman did something unpardonable. Standing in the dimly lit hallway with his legs spread firmly apart, Norman smacked Lily a great slap, right on her left cheek. For once, she could not think of one word to say. As a bright pink blotch spread over her face, Lily turned like a shot, ran to her little room up four steps and around the corner, and flung herself face down on her bed.

There she naturally cried. Who wouldn't? And since Mother was way down on the first floor in the kitchen, and Daddy was reading his newspaper on the second floor, no one was nearby to witness the terrible deed. So it seemed useless to run down the stairs to tell Mother or Daddy.

Let me tell you about those stairs. Every time Lily ran down those stairs – all thirty-six of them – and then climbed all the way back up, it seemed to her as if she was the first eight-year-old person in the world to conquer Mount Everest.

There was one time that Lily would have liked to forget about those stairs. One summer day while Mother was out shopping and Daddy was at work, and Norman was somewhere – who knew where – Lily had opened the heavy front door to the busy city street. Lily never left the safety of her house alone. Usually Mother or Norman went with her down the street to the store on the corner. But that day, Lily walked the short distance all by herself.

*Norman did something unpardonable*

She followed a lady into the store and then walked directly to the shelves full of candy. There was not one other person in that part of the store. No one at all. So it was very easy to reach up to the shelf and grab a bag of her favourite chocolate fudge. It just seemed to fly into her pocket. She did not even have to think about it. There it was, buried deep inside one pocket in her pink dress. All she had to do was walk down the aisle and out the door. And that's just what she did.

When Lily got home, she made it all worse. Her cheeks were bulging with chocolate as she opened and softly closed the front door of her house.

'Lily, where did you get the candy?' Mother asked. She just happened to be sitting near the front door when Lily got home.

'I found twenty-five cents on the sidewalk and went to the store and bought a bag of chocolates.'

Now one thing Lily had learned in her eight years of experience is that no one – no one – could fool Mother. Somehow, some way, Mother seemed to know exactly what Lily was thinking. Even Norman found it impossible to hide the truth from Mother. Of course, Lily's bulging cheeks blushing so red that her freckles disappeared, probably told Mother all she needed to know about Lily at that moment.

'Lily, go up to your room and get your Bible.' Mother's voice was so firm that each word sounded to Lily like the last word spoken to the last person on earth. And she remembered the sound of those words as she trudged up the stairs. The higher she climbed, the darker the stairs

4

were. Up the first fourteen stairs Lily climbed, then around to the next four stairs on the second floor landing.

Hanging on the wall over those stairs was a life-sized portrait of somebody's great-grandmother. Lily had never liked that picture. But that day, as she rested, panting and leaning on the railing, she looked up at that lady, whose mouth was usually a straight line. And then she looked away quickly, because the lady was grinning down at her. Her lips were turned up at the corners so that the tips of her teeth, like tiny light bulbs, gleamed in the gloomy darkness of the hallway. Not only that, the lady's black eyes were narrowed to slitty lines, open just enough so that she could look into Lily's wide open eyes.

Lily turned away and then swung her head, red curls bouncing, as fast as she could back to the portrait. This time the lady's mouth was a thin, straight line once more.

Not sure of exactly what she had seen, Lily climbed slowly up the four stairs, up fourteen more stairs, then around another corner and up four more stairs to her room.

By the time Lily reached her room, she wanted to spit out every bit of that chocolate, and she did – right into the crumpled shiny bag she had clutched all the way upstairs. Mother, she knew, would be waiting.

Her Bible firmly in both hands, Lily slowly climbed down those stairs. She had to pass that grim lady hanging on the wall, so when she came to the landing, she walked as close to the stair railing as she could. She kept her eyes down so as not to look at that narrow mouth in the picture. But with a little jerk of her head, she looked up as fast as she could. This time the lady's eyes were closed, and her mouth corners were turned way down, making long, deep lines from either side of her nose to the bottom of her pointy chin.

Then, all of a sudden, the lady stuck her tongue out with a jerk. Lily fairly flew down the rest of the stairs, which seemed to grow steeper as she ran. When she reached the bottom, she saw Mother sitting on the living room sofa. Her back was very straight, and she pointed to the seat beside her. Lily sat down carefully.

'Lily, open your Bible to Exodus 20. Here is a pencil.' She opened her Bible so quietly that the pages turned absolutely silently. For the next three minutes (which seemed like three hours, at least) Lily read the 'Thou shalt not steal' verse and then had to underline the verse in her Bible.

'Lily, you have hurt me very much. Go up to your room and think about what you have done.' Mother's voice seemed to come from the top of a tall tower. With those words bouncing up and down in her head, Lily climbed back up the stairs to her room.

This time, as she passed Great Grandmother's picture, Lily did not even look up, but she did not have to look because a very satisfied hum came from the lady's slitty mouth just as she ran past the gold framed picture hanging on the wall. She was wishing that Norman was home, just so that she could ask him to look at that picture. But when she thought more about it, she decided that Norman would just snicker and call her Silly.

The lady stuck her tongue out

Actually, Lily and Norman did not always fight with each other. Sometimes they got on quite well, especially when Norman had dreamed up some scheme and needed Lily to help him to pull it off. He was good at thinking up schemes, and he thought up a real peach of an idea one time when Mother had taken Lily and Norman to the park not far from their house. There they could jump on the rocks and hide from each other and play other games that Norman thought up while Mother sat on a bench nearby and watched. Of course, Mother was always watching. But it was possible to get lost in the park, if a person wanted to be lost. There were high rocky hills, full of twists and turns. But best of all, in the far corner of the park was a wide lake where sailboats romped and swayed on a good windy day.

Norman would have liked his own sailing boat. He just knew he could manage the sails. But Mother always said, 'You must wait until you are older and stronger.' So Norman had to be content to wait until that time, way in the future, when according to the way adults measure time, he was old enough to sail.

There was one especially happy thought that Norman played with inside his head for days and days at a time.

In the middle of the lake in the park was an island. And the only way to the island was a curved stone bridge that arched from the lakeside park and came down on the grassy shore on the other side. But because Mother never took them across the bridge, Norman wanted to do it. Actually he thought that Mother herself had never been across the bridge. But Norman had to know everything. So Norman decided that one day he would go to the park and find out what was hidden in the tall trees of the island in the lake. Just in case, he would take Lily with him. Just in case of what, Norman had no idea. But it seemed the thing to do.

It was almost time for school to begin again after the summer holidays, when Norman felt really brave. He called Lily, who was reading a book in her room.

When Lily heard what Norman wanted to do, she did not agree to go along – at least not for two or three minutes. Mother was out for a day of shopping, and Grandmother was asleep.

I forgot to mention Grandmother, but she and Grandfather lived with them all in the high three-storey house. Grandmother was a dear, cuddly person with eyeglasses that perched on her nose and puffs of piled-up white hair that had once been dark red just like Lily's hair. It had been Grandmother who took Lily by the hand when Mother insisted that Lily go to the corner store and tell the storekeeper she had taken candy and then give him twenty-five cents. Grandmother wanted to go with Lily because, as she said, 'That poor little thing! I'm sure she will never do it again. I'll just go along and help her explain to the storekeeper what happened.' Mother just closed her mouth and smiled, sort of.

But I must get back to my story. Norman finally talked Lily into trekking to the park to see what was on the island where no one had gone before – at least no one in their family. Lily decided she was not afraid. She felt sure that Norman would take care of her. So they left the house and walked briskly down the street. Norman's legs were longer than Lily's, so she had to take twice as many steps as Norman did, just to keep up. With each step, her large pink hair bow flapped up and down on her red curls.

'Normy—'

'Don't call me Normy!'

'Anyway, Nor-man, what do you think we will find on the island? Are there animals?

'Maybe.'

'Are there people there?'

'Maybe.'

'Should I be afraid?'

'Maybe. No more questions, Lily. I don't know. Just don't know.'

By this time, Lily had to take deep, puffy breaths because she almost had to run to keep up with Norman, and it was hard to talk. So she was just as happy not to ask any more questions.

It took twenty minutes to get to the park, and ten more minutes to find the curved stone bridge. By this time, Lily was beginning to feel quite guilty. She knew that Mother did not know where she and Norman were, and she suspected – no, she knew – that Mother would not like her and Norman to be so far from home on their own. But there you are! They were in the park. And that was that!

Norman, as usual, had very little to say, just 'Lily! Hurry up! Stop dragging your feet.' Lily's short, stubby legs could hardly move by the time they finally reached the stone bridge. She felt like sitting down for a little

rest. But Norman grabbed her arm and hurried Lily across, their feet tapping quickly on the stones. In ten giant steps, they were standing on the island.

The two of them stood still, looking at the thick, dark trees and bushes that grew down to the island edges like a great green wall. Five steps from the bridge in any direction would take them into the woods. Just in front of the bridge was one very narrow brown path studded with little rocks that led deep into the trees.

'Normy?'

'Don't call me—' Norman began.

'What will we do now? asked Lily in a tiny, squeaky voice.

'Well, I'm going to see what's in the woods. Coming?' And Norman took four or five crunching steps down the little rocky path. So what was Lily to do but follow him?

At first they plodded steadily along the path, but when the path grew even more narrow, and the trees grew thicker, Lily decided she was afraid. Of course, she did not say that word to Norman. She would not admit she was afraid because Norman would tease her, and Norman's teasing was no fun for Lily. So she shut her mouth tightly and walked on a bit more slowly than before, stubbing the toes of her brown shoes with every step. In fact, when the path turned suddenly to the right, she could not see Norman at all. At that point, the trees were growing so closely together that when she threw her head back and looked up as far as she could, there was no more blue sky up there. She saw only dark branches and thick leaves.

She began to think that she could no longer hear Norman's scrunchy feet on the path ahead. But maybe, just possibly, she thought she heard little quick steps behind her. She stood absolutely still and slowly counted to ten. 'Silly me,' she thought. 'It's just the breeze clicking through the bushes. I had better hurry along and catch up with Normy.'

But as soon as she took two steps, she thought she heard a giggle, light as air. Quick as a bunny, she whirled around. There was nothing there but the narrow path which now seemed to stop in mid-air just at the edge of the tall rustling bushes.

'Normy!' she yelled at the top of her voice. 'Normy!' But though she strained her ears and concentrated as hard as she could, she could hear no answering call. It was then that she knew for sure that she was definitely afraid.

Now, Lily had been afraid before. There was the time she had wandered away from Mother and Daddy down at the seashore and leaped into the water, paddling out to the building waves that grew much taller than her three-and-a-half feet. When an especially tall wave crashed over her and tumbled her round and round so that her head scraped the sandy bottom, it flashed into her frantic mind that she could not breathe and she did not know which way was up. Her fear was like a huge smothering wet blanket, but she fought her way to the surface, beating the heavy water with her wild arms churning all the way up. She had lived through that, so she had the smallest hope that she could get out of those woods and back home again, with or without Normy.

By then, Lily was so tired that her chubby knees could hardly bend, but she had the idea that she had better not just sit down because she would never get where she needed to be. So Lily gave herself a good talking to ('Just keep walking back in the direction you have come and soon you will be at the stone bridge, Silly.') and started off once again. There was only one path, after all. Surely she would soon see the bridge. So carefully she took one step, then another step, then another. She listened really hard, but there were no more giggling sounds behind her.

'I must be tired. That's all,' she whispered to the air.

She was tired, more tired than she had ever been before. But, like pulling her stubborn dog along on his leash, Lily pulled her feet along one step at a time. She mostly kept her eyes on the path because she did not want to trip and fall down. Normy was not there to pick her up.

When she finally did pay attention to the bushes along the path, it seemed to her that they were not just green. Yellowy flowers, just a few at first, grew among the leaves like cups sitting on green saucers, and some of the trees bloomed with purple and red clumps, like butterfly wings. The farther she walked, the more bright coloured blooms appeared in the leaves until there were more flowers than leaves. They grew so closely together by the time she had walked on for twenty minutes that Lily thought the flowers would squeeze together and cover the path. At last, she could not walk any farther because the flowers did indeed bloom more and more thickly until there was not even a narrow opening that Lily could walk through.

If Norman had been with her, he would have just bashed on through the wall of yellow, pink, orange, purple, and blue flowers. But Lily had begun to think that the flowers were trying to tell her something – like STOP!

Very carefully, she leaned forward to bury her nose in one especially orange bloom, plush with petals. It was silky to touch, and a most delicious scent tickled her nose. When she brushed away the tickle, tiny powdered sprinkles stuck to the end of her nose. You would think that those little bits would make her sneeze, but she did not even want to wipe them away. They made Lily feel pleasant and strangely strong, even vigorous. She felt as if she could walk on for hours.

14

Boldly, Lily swept aside a great petalled clump in a shower of golden sprinkles, and saw, a short way off, the edge of the deep blue-green lake. But soaring above the sparkly ripples of the water, taller than all the trees of the woods, stood a castle keep.

One thing you should know is that Lily loved books. In fact, on school days, when Mother gave her money to buy her lunch, she often bought a book instead. Sometimes on Saturdays, Mother took Lily to the great stone library in the city where she had her very own card for checking out books to take home. She would walk up and down the aisles of shelves and pull one book after another out of the rows of books of all sizes and colours. Soon she would have a pile of books so high she could hardly see over the top, and Mother would have to rescue her and help carry them for her. At home, in no time at all, she had read all those books, and back to the library she would go for more.

In one of those books, Lily had read about a stone castle far away in another country across the Atlantic Ocean. She remembered a picture that showed a tower taller than the walls of the grey castle. Narrow, slitty windows had been cut into the stones here and there all the way up to the top. All around the very top were square stone slabs, separated by keyhole openings where a person could stand and look far down to the trees below.

Lily could see that the great, grey stone tower in front of her looked almost exactly like the picture in the book. Daddy had explained to her that the tower in her book was called a 'keep'.

'What does it keep?' asked Lily.

'Sometimes prisoners, like a jail, and sometimes the master of the castle lived there,' explained Daddy.

'What prisoners?' asked Lily.

'People who came to attack the castle and were captured by the master's soldiers.'

This explanation only partly satisfied Lily because she was one of those people who *had* to understand. She would have asked lots more questions, but by that time Daddy was on another subject. She wished she had asked Daddy more questions when she stood in the flowery woods that day, looking up at the tower as far as she could see.

She called 'Normy!' with a little voice this time. But no answering call came back through the flowers or from the lake shore just beyond the tower.

Lily ran as fast as her stubby legs would carry her, down to the rocky shore. She scrunched down, scooped up a handful of water and drank a few drops just before they fell back onto the rocks. She was very thirsty.

As she stood and turned, Lily looked up as far as she could to the top of the tower, but out of the corner of her left eye, she saw the smallest movement at the bottom of the grey stone walls. Yes, there was an opening slowly widening next to a brilliant red flowered bush – it looked like a small, wooden door. This thick brown object did not swing open with a swoop. It barely moved, like leaves stirred ever so slightly by airy breaths. It made no noise, and to Lily's right and left and just behind her, she heard tiny giggles floating on the breezy trees.

Whirling around, she peered through the clumped flowers, but she could see nothing. She looked up at the tall trees, and still she saw nothing. So as she swung around, she looked cautiously at the open door and then flung her head back as far as she could, just in time to see at the top of the tower in one narrow slit of a window, for just one moment, a face.

Lily did not expect to see any face in these woods except Norman's. But the face in the high window was definitely not Norman's, though there was not enough time to actually see the face. In fact, Lily was not even sure what she had seen.

It became very quiet in the woods – no breezes, not even giggling. Lily blinked three times and looked up again to try to see the window at the tower top. No face filled the slitted window. But Lily did not want to stop looking because she was afraid she would miss something. She wondered if she could just keep looking up, that the face might return to the open window.

Whole minutes passed by, and Lily's bent neck began to feel achy, but she would not stop looking up. She decided that she *had* to look up as long as she could, and the instant she decided this, Lily truly did see someone looking at her from high in air, near the very top of the grey stony keep.

The face was framed with feathery white like the wings of a pearly dove, and this time it did not leave the window. Lovely eyes like deep blue starry sapphires looked right into Lily's pale blue eyes. And what is more amazing, Lily felt that she knew who was looking at her so kindly. She felt no surprise, no fear, and most of all, no doubt at all that she must get up to the top of the soaring tower to see the whole person who looked down at her from such a terrible height.

It was then that Lily realised she had not thought about Norman for a long time. If only Normy could see those beautiful glittering eyes at the top of the tower. She thought about calling his name again, but she had decided that with or without Norman, she must climb up to the top of the castle keep.

Lily walked quickly to the open doorway at the bottom of the grey stone tower of the castle keep. As she drew closer to the brown door, she heard a little voice inside her head that chirped, 'Don't climb the stairs. Don't climb up to the castle keep.' She turned around once and saw on a tree branch just out of reach, a small black bird who seemed to chirp at her in a decidedly argumentative tone. But Lily did not believe in talking birds, so she turned quickly and peered into the open doorway.

'It looks all right,' she told herself. But two steps inside the tower she stepped quickly away from the little door just in time, for it closed behind her with a determined, thump. Lily had heard that sound before in Mother's voice, when she had made up her mind about what Lily should or should not do. One could not argue with Mother when her voice had such a final sound.

Once inside the bottom of the tower, Lily stood still for ten whole seconds, which she counted inside her head. The room was only dimly lit from above, where one of the narrow windows opened to the woodland air.

*Don't climb the stairs*

So shadowy was the room where Lily stood hardly daring to move, that she could see just four stone steps next to the closed wooden door now firmly shut.

Lily turned and thought about opening the door to look outside. Maybe Norman had found the tower too and did not see the door in the stones. But when she felt along the edge of the smooth wood, there was no handle, no keyhole, nothing. And remembering that the door had opened to the inside, Lily knew at that moment, she was one of those prisoners that Daddy told her about – she was standing in an empty room at the bottom of a castle keep. Only the memory of a shining face with starry eyes kept Lily from bursting into tears. However, she sat down on the lowest step and did not move for quite a long time, her arms and legs limp and her heart beating faster than she had ever felt it before.

How long Lily sat on the cool stones, she did not know. But she did not move until the sound of a musical air swirled lightly about her red curls and settled comfortably with the lightest touch on the very top of her head. It felt like the nicest touch of a soft hand, and Lily was sure that her curly head was ringed about with the purest, sweetest music she had ever heard. She tried to hum the tune, but because she had never heard such a melody before, she could not even come close to humming the same tune. She believed that if she could think very hard, maybe she could tell where the music was coming from. So thinking and listening with all her might, Lily began to pick out word-like notes that quite clearly sounded like 'Come up. Come to me.'

Up! Up how? 'Up the stairs, Silly,' she whispered to the sweet air. Turning around on her stony seat on the first step, she saw only three more steps which did not appear to go farther up than the fourth one. Well, she knew what Norman would do. He would dash up the four steps, no matter what. So that is what she did.

The first three steps were pretty easy to climb, but when four more steps appeared to curve around to the left, Lily was uncertain about what to do. She picked up her right foot, intending to place it firmly on the fourth step, but when she put her foot down, the step wiggled, and she almost tumbled down to the bottom. Bracing her right hand on the rounded stone wall of the tower, Lily balanced herself while the step beneath her foot moved smoothly up and down and then from side to side. She felt as if she was trying to climb up one of those waves in the surf at the beach.

For several minutes, Lily struggled to drag her left foot up to the weaving fifth step, and every time she thought she had her foot fixed to that step, it wiggled up and down, making her foot bounce whappita, whappita, on the stone. The sixth step was jiggling from side to side, jerking dangerously. With all her strength, Lily put her weight on the sixth step and picked up her right foot as high as it would go. It took all her concentration to find the step and as fast as she could, reach up to the seventh step before the sixth threw her all the way down to the bottom.

By this time, Lily was beginning to feel discouraged, to say the least. But when her foot found the solidly quiet seventh step, she sank down for a minute or two to catch her breath. She was amazed to find that when she looked down the six stairs she had struggled to climb, the stairs looked perfectly still. In fact, she was beginning to feel a little foolish, thinking she had only imagined the wildly careening steps.

But when Lily stood up, turned and carefully put her foot on the eighth step, it pitched her foot off and left her balancing on the other foot like a tight-rope walker leaning this way and that. Lily felt a bit angry, and determined to reach the top somehow, some way, she swayed and leaped, pulled and bobbed, up the continually moving steps, trying to brace herself stiff-armed, along the curving grey stone walls. Some of the steps she thought she never would find with her feet. She was thankful that every seventh step was quite still. So she rested each time she came to the seventh of each set of seven steps reaching up to a higher level in the tower.

She did not rest long on each seventh step, though, because inside her head she heard a voice every time that sounded much like Norman's saying, 'Come on, Lily. Keep up.' Weaving in and out of those words like a ribbon of music was that melody that she could not hum, no matter how hard she tried.

She stopped counting how many steps she climbed, but she thought she had rested on a seventh step at least six times. Surely, she thought, she was almost to the top of the tower. She had passed at least twelve of the narrow, slitty windows, but she had been too busy struggling to keep her balance on the stone steps to stop and look down below at the ground. So, how far up she was, she did not know.

Just the time that Lily supposed she was surely almost as high as the sky, and leaning her head far back to see if the steps were finally ending in the dim distance above her, she came to the end of the stairs. Fortunately, the last step was a seventh step.

With both feet firmly fixed to the quiet step, she waited. She did not know what she was waiting for, but she had the idea that someone was standing just beyond the wall at the top of the steps. In fact, that wall, just in front of Lily, was very like the wall of tightly growing flowers in the woods. Then she had swept those blooms aside with her arm to part the way through to the other side. So Lily lifted her arm and lightly touching the wall just there at the seventh step, she watched as the wall swung open and she was looking beyond the stones to a starlit room.

The room appeared to grow higher, widening upward to a great domed circle as Lily stepped inside. At first she could not see clearly any object but the widening walls and high soaring ceiling. When her eyes began to be used to the soft light of a starlit evening, Lily found she could pick out one or two brilliant stars so bright, so piercing, she could not look at them for long. These lights multiplied and then moved airily about the large room until there were so many bright spots that it seemed to Lily that all the lightning bugs she and Normy had ever collected in jars each summer had been let loose to dance before her delighted eyes. Lily wanted to just sit and watch the ballet of the lights, but she saw no chair in the room to sit on. She had little time to think about this, because there was no doubt that someone was waiting very near.

'I am glad you climbed up to me, Little One.' The voice seemed to float on the air and come from deep inside her mind at the same time. 'I have waited for you, and for Norman, too. You are tired. Here, let me help you.' With that, strong arms gathered Lily up so that she could lean her weary head against a pillowy breast. She did not speak, but lay peacefully in the arms of a Being whose brightness was like the dancing stars.

When Lily found her voice, she asked, 'Are you the master of the castle keep?'

'No, Little One. I am one of many who serve him night and day.'

'Why am I here?' Lily asked.

'Because the Master of the castle keep chose you.'

'But how does he know me?' Lily wanted to know.

'He knew you before you were born.'

'He did?' Lily did not understand this, but she suspected that eventually she would understand everything.

'He does. He knows all about you.'

'Does he know Normy, too?' Lily wondered.

'Yes,' sang the music of the voice, giving Lily a most delicious feeling.

'But why would he choose me – and Normy too?'

'The Master loves you both, and he forgives you all. Now you can truly be his children.'

*Will I always be his child?*

'Will I always be his child?'

'Yes. The Master's son gave all he had to make you his child, so the Master will never give you up. Now it is time to go to your father and mother. The Master has guided them to the bridge in the park. They are waiting anxiously for you both. I will take you to the bottom of the steps.'

Woven in and out of the Being's words was the melody that Lily could not hum when she was outside the tower. But when she tried to hum inside her head while she rested cosily in the comforting arms, the melody slipped smoothly into her mind. This discovery made her smile, and she looked up into heavenly blue eyes.

Lily was carried softly down to the little door at the bottom of the tower where it swung open to the flowered woods. She was set gently on her feet, and a strong soft hand touched her curly head. 'Be careful, Little One.'

'Will I see you again?' she wanted to know.

'Of course.'

Lily needed to think about this 'Of course' very quietly and carefully.

And then there was Norman. 'Where was he?' she thought, as she sank down on a mossy patch by a hedge thick with yellow and purple petals.

Sweetness like a cloud settled about her weary head, and rested on her shoulders, while Lily fell into a delicious sleep. What she saw on the inside of her eyelids were dark blue eyes like jewels, looking far and deep inside, right down to her heart.

# he Castle Keep too

As it happened, while Lily was brushing golden dust from her red eyelashes, Norman was skipping saucer-shaped stones across the rippled lake. He walked along the shore kicking pebbles like marbles and began to feel hot and sweaty. The lake looked so inviting that he peeled off his damp shirt, yanked off his shoes, hid his glasses in one shoe, and waded into cool blue water up to his chin. Then, seeing the short distance he would need to swim to reach the other shore, he pushed off the sandy bottom with his right foot and stroked strongly away.

No sooner had his arms stroked three times and his legs kicked six times than he felt the water bouncing him higher and powerfully into the building waves. Looking up through drops that streamed from his floppy hair, he saw that the far shore was much farther away than when he had waded into the lake.

A boy who was less brave might have felt a growing knot of fear beginning to fill up his stomach. But Norman, who could be quite logical when he put his mind to it, simply stopped swimming and turned around, kicking his feet and weaving his arms in a circle. In fact, he flapped his arms so strongly around and around, that he could not seem to stop. He wanted to stop, but he could not. He tried to stop, but nothing he did, even weaving his arms in the opposite direction, could stop him from twirling faster and faster.

As he whirled in the choppy waves, he began to feel that he was sinking. He tried to rear up in the water so he could see how close he was to the shore. But when he looked to the shore he had just left, he saw only a silver mist so thick that he had only a vague impression of which direction the island was. What was more, Norman could see the sky above him growing dark and dense.

'Now I'm afraid,' gulped Norman.

At the same time, he felt the waves sweep higher and higher as if many great wings were fanning the water into towering heights. His eyes filled with water, so that he was not really certain just what he was looking at. Was it his imagination, or were there lights bobbing on the rising watery mountains? Lights flitted and glittered, diving and leaping through the waves. Two of the littlest lights buzzed and twittered just under his nose. Norman half expected them to jump right into his gasping mouth. He wanted to clamp his lips together so they could not slip inside, but when he tried, he choked for air.

Kicking his legs as hard as he could to keep his head above the cresting waves, he stared at one especially large, white brilliance. It rode high on a wave that curled above him, and he had a growing feeling that this flashing brightness was looking at him, even knew him by name.

At the very moment when Norman began to think he could not hold up his head, he heard a sound moving across the wildly careening waves. It was music! And each note leaped up one side of a heaving wave and slid down the other side, playing and bouncing against each other. The melody was so purely beautiful that Norman decided he was not exactly afraid after all.

Just when a tight cluster of sweet notes like a bouncing ball seemed about to leap into his open mouth, Norman felt two powerful arms anchored under his struggling arms and legs. This so surprised him that he jerked his head back to look up as high as he could, while trying to wipe his streaming eyes with his soggy fists. What Norman saw was a face, brilliant – kind.

Norman had been about to cry, 'Help!' But he felt completely secure, cradled in warm arms. In fact, it was three whole seconds before he realised that the water valleys and mountains had flattened to a perfect mirror. More than that, no mist hid the two shores of the calm lake. As for the brightness that held him tenderly, billowing out behind the Being, spread wide and tall above them both, were two densely feathered, white wings. Norman blinked twice and then knew that somehow he was once again standing on the island shore where thick trees crowded close to the water's edge.

'How– why– who– ?' Norman stammered.

'I saw you struggling,' sang the Brilliance. 'My Master knows you, my child.'

'Who is the Master?' asked Norman.

'The one I serve, night and day.'

'Does he know Lily, too?'

'Yes, and your mother and father. He has chosen to rescue you because he loves you and forgives all the wrong things you have ever done.'

'Why would he do that – for me?' Norman found this idea amazing.

'The Master has a son who agreed to be punished for what you have done.'

Norman could not understand all of the wonderful words, but he wished with all his heart he could tell the Master's son that he loved him.

'You can. Now it is time to return to Lily. Just walk straight into the woods until you see a castle keep.'

'What's that?'

'Lily will explain it to you.'

Norman looked in the direction of the woods and then turned to thank his rescuer, but he saw only the blue sky and a calm little lake. So shirt buttoned and shoes tied, he walked away from the rocky shore and entered the woods. As he walked, he breathed sweet air that rose from thickly flowered bushes. He began to think that poor Lily was probably wandering from tree to tree, tears falling in wide streams down her freckles to her chin.

'Poor kid,' he thought, as his path turned and opened out to a wide clear place in the woods.

There in the centre of the clearing rose the castle keep. And near the bottom of the tower, leaning comfortably against soft, velvety petals, was Lily. The corners of her mouth curled up, and she hummed a little purring song.

With that, Lily felt a finger on her nose. 'Lily, come on. Dad and Mother are waiting at the stone bridge. What's this sprinkly gold stuff?' Norman brushed away the sweet flowery dust.

'How do you know Mother and Dad are waiting?'

'I just know.'

'Are they angry?' Lily asked, looking up where Norman's head filled the sky. Lily saw her own face reflected in both round, clear lenses of his glasses.

'Don't think so,' Norman said in his manliest voice, as he gently helped Lily to her feet. They walked carefully to the edge of the tall trees.

'I climbed to the top of the tower. Did you see it?' Lily almost did not mention what happened inside the tower. She did not like it when Norman laughed at her. But he did not laugh.

'I swam in the lake. Almost didn't get back to the shore. Got awful tired. Had help. It was an ang— I'll tell you later.'

Lily looked up at Norman's face very closely. He had said more words than he had ever said to her all at once ever before. When Norman took Lily's hand as they stepped on the curved stone bridge and walked across together, Lily said, 'I love you, Normy.'

For once, Norman did not say, 'Don't call me Normy.'

And all the way home through the park, Daddy and Mother held their hands as if they would never let go of Lily and Norman.

THE END

# he Castle Knight

'Ninety-six . . . ninety-seven . . . ninety-eight . . . ninety-nine . . . ONE HUNDRED!' Lily shouted the 'one hundred' as loudly as she could. And then she yelled, 'Ready! Or! Not! Here! I! Come!' – each word separately, so there was no doubt that she was ready. Lily had been hugging a small tree, and her eyes were closed so tightly that her cheeks almost touched her eyebrows. She loved hide-and-seek.

The reason she had learned to count to one hundred in the first place was so that Normy, her big brother, would finally let her play games with him and his friends. Usually they had said, 'No, Lily! You're too little.' Normy finally promised she could play when she could count to one hundred. She was eight years old and had been counting to one hundred since her sixth birthday. So there!

Just as she let go of her tree, she heard very fast, pattering steps behind the park's stone wall. She leapt into the air as high as she could and saw, for one half a second, the green hair ribbon on top of Crystal's black bobbing head.

Crystal was her new friend. She was eleven and knew absolutely everything. She and her brother, Beau, lived down the hall on the fifth floor of their apartment building right in the middle of London, where apartments were not apartments. They were flats. Lily did not understand how an apartment could be flat, but she was sure that one day this idea would be clear, along with all the answers to her many other questions.

Two months before, Lily's dad had announced at the dinner table that he had to go to England to work there for his company. 'Well, kids, your mother and I have to move to London for a year. Anyone want to come with us?'

'Sure.' Norman was a boy of few words.

'Me, too? You wouldn't leave me here?' Lily's voice rose to a squeak.

'No, Lily. We want to be together. All of us,' Daddy assured her.

So Mother packed – for days and days. Lily wanted to take more of her stuff than there was room to fit into her biggest bag. It was just too difficult making choices – what to leave and what to take. But Norman had no problem. He was all packed in one day, and he showed up at the front door with one small suitcase when it was time to leave for the airport.

Of course, Lily had flown on an airplane once before, when the whole family had gone to visit her Aunt Laura in Florida. But this time, she knew she would have to sit in the same seat for at least seven hours while the plane flew all night long. Now, Lily had never sat still one hour, let alone seven hours. Also, she was so excited by the time they all arrived at the airport, that she wiggled all the way from the door, up the elevator, through the crowded terminal to the gate and then on to the airplane.

Meanwhile, Norman walked through the crowds as if he flew from America to another country every day. On the plane, he slouched neatly in his seat and played a little electronic game, which he always managed to win.

As for Lily, flying all the way across the Atlantic Ocean with Norman sitting on her left, she sat next to the window and sputtered and stewed. 'What if I don't meet anybody to play with? What if I don't like my new school? What if—'

'Lily!' said Norman, 'Stop what-if-ing. Think about this. England is full of castles – like your castle on the island in the park.'

Lily had told Norman all about meeting her angel at the top of the castle keep on the island in the city park. And Norman had not even laughed. She had the feeling that he was not telling her something. But that was just Norman. He probably had lots of secrets – secrets that not even Mother knew.

So on the airplane, when Norman said the word 'castle', Lily should have been ready for what she saw. She had been staring out the window at a little white light winking at the end of the plane's long silvery wing.

When Normy said 'castle', a giant, white feathery wing flapped slowly in great sweeping strokes just where the silver one had been. Lily went limp all over and grabbed Norman's arm. She had seen wings like that before.

'Normy! Look!' She pulled so hard on Norman's arm that he almost fell over into her seat. 'The wing, the wing.'

But when Norman looked, he saw only the long silver wing of the plane, its white light blinking in the dark night sky.

'Silly Lily. Go to sleep.' Norman scrunched down in his seat and was soon fast asleep. But Lily sat with wide open eyes, staring out the window to the endless stars.

So you can imagine how tired Lily was when the plane finally dropped out of the sky and thump-touched the long runway at the airport near London. In fact, after they got off the plane, Mother had to remind her three times to keep up. 'Just put one foot in front of the other, Lily. We'll soon be in our new home.'

But they had to walk through the terminal down endless hallways, past piles of suitcases and hundreds of passengers waiting to get on airplanes. Men in uniform wanted to know what they had packed in all their luggage, and they all waited in ragged lines of people stretching so far that Lily could not see where they ended. So finally Lily just sat down on one of their suitcases and nodded off. Norman was bright-eyed and alert, of course.

An hour or so later, they all arrived in a van, with their pile of luggage, at their new home. It was a beautiful flat on the fifth floor of a row of white houses that had four flats on each level. Before Lily fell into her new bed in her very own room, she stood at her window and saw a little square of green down below, dotted with pink and yellow flowers all around the edges. Her own park, she thought as she climbed into her bed, and was soon deep in sleep as the dawning sun began to light the city.

Soon after they had moved into their London flat, Norman and Lily met Crystal and Beau. They all liked each other from the start. Crystal was eleven, like Norman, and Beau was eight, like Lily.

She liked Beau especially. He was funny, and Lily spent hours giggling at Beau's stories. He was only one inch taller than Lily and had a wide, quick smile and gleaming hair like gold that he combed thickly across his forehead.

Crystal was tall for her age with straight, swingy black hair that she wore swooped up on the sides and tied with a ribbon on top of her head. She talked very little, just like Norman, and they spent many semi-silent hours strolling, sitting, playing games, or rowing on the lake in a huge park a short ride from their flat.

The day the four of them were playing at hide-and-seek in the park, Lily's mother had spread luncheon on a blanket on the grass. In between the sandwiches, they talked about what they would do the coming weekend. Lily's father had promised a trip to the country to see a castle. They chattered, at least Lily and Beau chattered, and planned their trip. Once Norman said the word 'castle', and Lily felt a flutter in the centre of her back that skipped and tickled beneath her shirt, right up to her fat red curls at the back of her neck.

The night before their trip into the country, Lily lay in bed with her eyes wide open. Twice she heard a light, fluffy sound like a tiny hum just outside her window. When she looked to where her blue curtains framed the starry sky, she saw a whirr of white wings waving in the night air, and she smiled quietly to herself. She decided not to mention the wings to any of the others, even Beau. Crystal had already said four times, 'Lily, you're weird.'

After breakfast the next morning, they jumped into a van that Dad had rented for the weekend. Lily liked the van because it was big enough so that everyone could sit next to a window. Usually on trips, she would be stuck between two people in the back seat of a car. Lily hated to miss anything.

It took an hour just to get out of the city, past the rows of houses and office buildings, and then finally leave the crowded highway. When Daddy drove down a ramp and turned on to a country road, Lily got so excited she poked Beau in the ribs every time she wanted to get his attention. Fortunately Beau did not mind. But when they turned down a narrow lane, hardly wide enough for their van, even Norman sat up straight. Through the trees and hedges that crowded both sides of the lane, they could just begin to see the grey stones and turrets of a castle, piled high on a green, sloping hill.

'It's my castle!' Lily squealed.

'I don't think it's *yours* Lily.' Crystal's voice sounded just a bit annoyed.

'Lily just loves castles,' Beau offered. He always took Lily's side, even when Crystal told him once that he was just a baby, like Lily. But they were all so excited that they soon forgot to argue whose castle it was. So as soon as the van stopped, they jumped out and ran toward a wide wooden bridge high above a dark moat filled with murky water. The moat was wide and stretched as far as they could see all around the bottom of the castle.

'Children, slowly. We have all day,' Dad called. 'Stay together. Norman, take care of the others.' Dad's voice sounded far away by the time the four children raced across the bridge and fairly flew through a narrow passage, walled on both sides and above and below with rough stones. They burst into a wide open courtyard where across wide, flat stones, a small sign over a doorway on the far side announced: GALLERY.

'What do they keep in a gallery?' Lily wanted to know.

'When our father brought us here two years ago, the gallery was full of swords and armour and pictures of really old people,' Crystal explained. 'I'd rather see the maze outside on the other side of the castle wall.'

'But I want to see everything,' Lily said, and whisked inside the gallery door. As she crossed the threshold, she had the funniest feeling that her shoes were acting peculiar. A quick look down at her feet stopped her in her tracks. Her shoelaces were flapping wildly in the air.

'Normy!'

But Norman, Crystal and Beau had gone, and she could not make her laces lie down. She leaned over to grab them, but no matter how hard she tried to press them to her shoes, they only tickled her palms. And besides, her blood had rushed to her head, so she had to stand up. Then she tried running. The gallery was long with a towering ceiling painted with flags, each one with different colours, shapes and designs – stripes or crosses or animals like lions and antlered deer. It was fortunate that there was no one about, because Lily picked up her feet and raced down the polished wooden floor, every step echoing like hollow taps through the long room.

As she ran, Lily passed faces framed in gold, hanging on the walls. But she came to a squealing stop in front of a tall, lovely portrait. Inside the heavy gold frame was a face she knew at once. It was her angel, the one from the castle keep who had picked her up and held her gently. He had told her he would see her again, and there he was.

Lily stood a long time, her feet still at last, her laces lying quietly on her shoe tops. In fact, she felt as if her shoes were nailed to the floor. The angel's eyes looked deeply into Lily's eyes and she could not move, even if she had wanted to move.

Just when she thought maybe she should go find the others, she heard a soft clinka-chink at the very end of the gallery. Dragging her eyes away from her angel, she looked far to her left. There, standing powerfully at the far end of the gallery, his head and sides covered with shiny armour, was a horse. His long face was hidden behind a carved silver mask that had two round spaces for his brown eyes which seemed to look in Lily's direction. His ears stood up straight inside their protecting metal ears so that Lily could just see their velvety tips, and his mouth and muzzle seemed to breathe just below the end of his silver mask. He was the biggest horse Lily had ever seen. And, of course, she had never seen a horse wearing armour.

But she almost stopped breathing when she saw, sitting in the horse's carved saddle, a giant armoured knight. Lily knew a knight when she saw one. She had a book at home about King Arthur and his knights of the round table. There were no pictures, but this knight looked exactly the way her book described Sir Lancelot. He was her favourite.

Just like Lancelot, this knight wore armour that shone like polished silver and completely covered him, arms, legs and all. And on his head he wore a helmet topped with a brilliant white feathered plume that fell thickly from the crown down to his broad shoulders. Even more amazing, two glittering sparks flashed from the narrow eye slits in the helmet's visor, directly into Lily's eyes.

Slowly, carefully placing each foot down softly on the wooden floor, Lily walked through the gallery toward the waiting knight. At last, she stood next to one armoured foot that rested in its right stirrup, and looked up as far as she could. She had to crunch her neck and lean far back, and when she did, she saw that the knight's visor was open, hinged up. His face inside the helmet was lit like lightning, and his sapphire eyes looked down, straight into Lily's pale blue eyes – and winked.

Just then, Lily heard Beau calling her. No, surely the knight had not winked at her. But she had no time to think about it, and she could hardly explain her knight to the others. She looked back over her shoulder once as she raced back down the long gallery to meet Beau. This time, the knight's visor was closed over his shining face, and she had just a moment to see that a white feather at the end of his helmet's plume fluttered once.

Beau was standing in the doorway. 'Lily, we've been waiting for you. The others are out behind the castle and there's a huge maze, and Norman and Crystal want us to go inside and see who can find the way out first, and I said I would come to get you, and what were you doing in here?' Beau usually talked in stringy sentences, and what with running outside with Lily and talking the whole time, he was quite out of breath by the time they reached the maze where Norman and Crystal were waiting.

Norman was reading a sign on a post next to the maze whose long straight hedge walls stretched far to the right and far to the left. The entrance was an opening between two square hedges that reached above their heads so high that they could not see the leafy tops.

Norman read slowly, 'Sir Eliott Enthwistle designed and grew this maze to amuse his bride whom he married on January 1, 1499. Only one person has ever discovered the secret pattern of the maze and found his way out without a map. That person is the knight whose statue stands at the end of the long gallery in the castle. He entered the maze on December 25, 1500, at seven o'clock in the morning and walked back through this opening at twelve noon the same day.'

'Oh, boy! Let's go!' Beau was springing into the air, higher and higher while Crystal tried to hold him down.

'First,' said Norman, slowly and deliberately, trying to smooth down his flighty hair, 'we have to have a plan. Who is going into the maze first?'

'Me. Pick me,' Beau was almost flying. 'I'm not scared.'

'I'm not afraid either, and I don't need a map.' Lily said softly. She had a secret.

'I think that Lily should go in first if she's so eager to try,' Crystal said. 'We'll wait here so we can rescue her when she gets lost.'

Lily simply smiled and walked through the hedge opening without even looking back. She did not want to explain to the others why she was so excited. But inside her pink shirt, Lily's heart was beating so rambunctiously that she was afraid the others could see it thumping on the outside.

*. . . through the hedge opening without looking back*

Once Lily was inside, the path between the high hedge walls turned left then right then left again, so that very soon Lily had not a clue which direction she was walking. Not only that, but the sun had not climbed above the tops of the maze, and she walked in shadows. She walked in whatever direction the maze took her, sometimes coming to a wall of hedge that blocked her path. Then she would have to turn around and walk back to where she had seen an opening.

At first, she could hear a voice or two. And once Norman called, 'Where are you, Lily?' His voice was far away. And even his last word – 'Lily' – had faded away before he got to 'ly', and after that Lily did not hear another sound.

How many times Lily turned around, walked back and forth, left and right, she did not know. She had started out counting the turns, but soon she could not remember if she had made twelve turns or twenty turns. Once when Lily looked up, she saw the sun exactly between the flat tops of the hedges. But two more twists in the path and two more blank hedge walls, and the sun was gone down behind the hedge tops.

Lily had just about decided that this maze was no longer fun. Maybe that was because she was hungry and tired, and there was no place to sit and rest, just the dusty path. But Lily refused to call for help. Besides, who would hear her? She had not heard a sound for a long while except the steady pad-pad-pad of her shoes as she walked. She had made up her mind that no matter what happened, she would not be afraid. She had a secret, and she hugged it inside where fluttery tickles began in her throat and dived down to the bottom of her stomach after every turn in the path.

After all, Lily had looked into the eyes of her knight, and he had winked at her. Yes, she was sure. He had definitely winked. What's more, she had decided that his shining face was very like the face of her angel in the castle keep.

So she walked on and on, turning with the path. It did begin to seem that she was having to turn back more often than she had at first. In fact, two or three short steps in any direction brought her smack up against a solid green hedge wall. It was all quite frustrating. How would she ever find her way out if she could not get past those towering walls? Besides, the space between the hedges began to grow dusky with long shadows.

If she were actually as tall as her own shadow stretching down the path, she could have looked over the top of the hedge.

'I'm so tired,' Lily said out loud as she leaned against the hedge wall. Just then, a short leafy sprig leaped out of the hedge and stuck its green end in her left ear, twirling round and round. Lily tried to catch it, but the

sprig was faster than her fingers, and she leaped across the path to the other side. But that hedge bounced her back to the other side. Ga-lump, whamp – the hedge walls pushed her back and forth along the path, the tiny, green leaves softly singing, 'Skritch, skritch,' and Lily could not gather her breath to shout for help. Faster and faster the hedges pushed her along the path which stretched far into the dim distance. No end wall blocked her headlong rush, and Lily gave herself up to the plunging hedges.

At just the moment when her heart grew so large in her stomach that she felt like an enormous red ball, the hedges slowed and stopped, leaving Lily sitting in the middle of the path.

In front of her stood a hedge wall at least as wide as the hedge was tall. All around Lily was quiet dusk as she rested, too weak to move. Weakly she whispered, 'Whatever will I do?'

'I will help you.'

Lily had been resting her head in her hands in a bit of a daze and was not sure she had actually heard the words. They sounded like music, and when her mind finally began to work, she knew even before she looked that standing near her in the dark was her knight.

'Come, little one.'

When Lily's eyes got used to the shadowed evening, she saw that the hedge wall had parted in two down the middle, swinging back on either side like heavy doors. She stood next to her knight in a stone doorway of a quiet courtyard. On either side of the doorway, hanging on the walls were flaming torches which cast long, flickering shadows in front of them. Inside there were twelve fat stone columns in a long line on each of the four sides of the paved square. In the middle of the square was a great stone fountain, round like a bowl. It stood on carved stone legs, and from the bowl, trickling streams of water flowed from stony flower petals, down into a quiet pool.

'The falling water sounds like music,' Lily said to the cool night air. She looked far up to the deepening sky where the face of her tall knight gleamed down at her like a star. As they stood together in the quiet, Lily knew that she was safe at last.

While the stillness around Lily and her knight was full of shadows, his face shone so brightly that the two of them stood in a circle of golden light. So Lily, who was a very curious person, could see every inch of silver armour that covered him from his feet to the top of his head. Wrapped around his waist was a blue silky sash with gold thread woven in curled designs at the edges. But in the wide silk ends hanging down to his knees were golden letters which spelled TRUTH. Carefully, Lily reached her finger to touch the letters and felt the gold thread, sewn thick and stiff.

'It's beautiful, Sir,' Lily whispered.

Above his sash, the knight wore across his wide chest, heavy silver armour carved with wavy lines that all pointed to the place just above his heart where the word PURE was spelled in gold letters. On his feet, the knight wore silver shoes, each one stamped in gold with the word PEACE from ankle to toe. He carried in his left hand a great shield almost as tall as Lily. It was carved with arrows, all pointing to the centre and the word FAITH in straight tall letters. And on his right hip he wore a heavy, long golden sword, engraved with letters of a language that Lily had never seen before. But two words were written larger than the rest, and they spelled THE WORD.

Lily could not take her eyes off the powerful knight, who stood beside her. She wished she were taller so that she could see all of his splendid armour. As if he heard her thinking her wish, the knight led Lily to a flat stone near the fountain and sat down. Now Lily could look into his eyes, and she thought she had never seen eyes so clear and deeply blue as his. Above his face, covering his head, the knight wore a shining helmet. Lily was just tall enough to see near the top, at the crown of the helmet, a carved lamb, ringed with letters that spelled SALVATION. And from the very top flowed a plume of sparkling white feathers.

'I knew you would come. I was not afraid to enter the maze,' whispered Lily.

'Do not ever be afraid, Lily. I will always protect you.' The knight spoke gently, while Lily stood at his knee, unable to take her eyes from his glowing face. 'But you must arm yourself, too. As you grow, there will be many battles for you to fight and win. Now, Lily,' said the knight, as he stood up, rising tall above her, 'kneel down.'

And taking his golden sword from its belt, he waved it in the air three times and touched first Lily's right

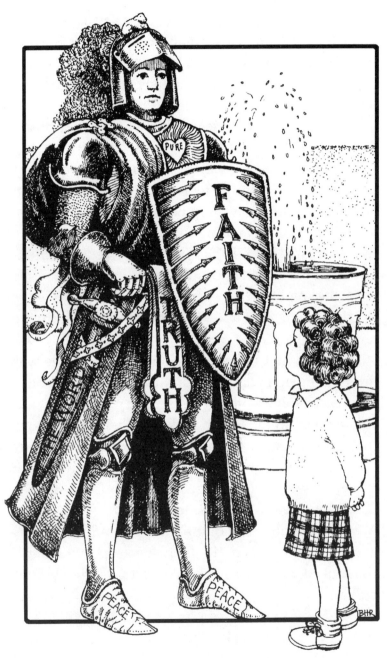

*I knew you would come*

shoulder and then her left, as softly as a feather. 'I name you Child of Truth. Now stand up, Little One. It is time to return to your family and friends.'

At first, Lily could think of nothing to say, which hardly ever happens.

'Thank you, Sir. But the words – what do they mean?' Lily just had to understand.

'Think, Lily. Think.' With this, the knight looked deeply into Lily's eyes. Then he took her hand in his silver one and led Lily to his waiting horse. The horse in all his armour had been standing so quietly in the doorway of the courtyard that Lily had no idea it was there. But its great powerful right hoof stroked the stones three times when the knight swung up into the saddle, reached down to Lily with his arm and floated her to a seat in front of him.

Then the knight nudged his horse into a gentle walk through the open doorway and into the maze. As they rode, each hedge wall that crossed the path swung open before them. In the time it took for Lily to count to ten, she and her knight reached the final turn in the maze. As gently as a knight could, who was covered from head to toe in heavy armour, he set Lily on her feet just before the path turned to the outside.

'May I ask just one question? I've seen you before, haven't I?' Lily asked. 'In the castle keep in the park?' She looked up as far as she could to see the knight's brilliant face.

'I told you I would see you again, Lily. I will always be near you,' said the knight.

54

Lily took two steps toward the opening in the outside hedge and looked back to see her knight for one last time. But he was gone, and all around Lily was thick darkness so that she had to feel her way along the last hedge wall. The little hedge leaves stroked her hand, moving it along until she stepped, at last, into the outside garden where the lighted castle wall towered above her.

'Lily! What happened?' They were all talking at once – Daddy, Mother, Norman, Crystal and Beau. 'We've been calling and calling.'

'Dad has been walking up and down in the maze for hours, looking for you.' Mother was so glad to see Lily that she could not be truly angry.

'But I told you I could find my way out,' Lily began. She knew she would have a very difficult time explaining her adventure this time.

'I'll try to explain.' And she did try, all the way back in the van to their London flat. Of course, she left out some parts of her story. Her knight was her knight. And for a while, Lily would keep that part to herself.

THE END

# he Castle Kite

THE NIGHT OF NORMAN'S THIRTEENTH BIRTHDAY, Dad gave him the one gift he wanted – a camera. All around the smooth silver camera in its box were rows of round coloured lenses that could be attached to the camera's telescoping lens on the front. Deeper inside the box was a soft camera case and a special red strap for holding the camera around his neck. Norman was – as he said – on the moon about his new treasure with all the extras.

The next day, Norman sat down with Dad, and together they read the fat instruction book – all about which lenses to use in bright sunlight and which ones to use on cloudy days. Lily wanted to look at the lenses, too. It was all Norman could do not to shout at her. He was usually a boy of few words, but at moments like this, Norman's hair would stand straight up on the top of his head.

'Lily! Don't touch. Don't ever touch my camera or the lenses,' he said, trying to smooth down his flighty hair.

'But Normy—'

'I wish you would not call me Normy – ever again. I am thirteen years old.'

'OK! OK! Nor-man. I just wanted to see the pretty coloured glass things.'

Sometimes Lily could be really annoying. And Norman was still getting used to the idea of being patient with his little sister. He truly did love Lily. But she could be a pain. There were days when Lily talked in long, streaky sentences without stopping. She had questions and opinions about everything, but she could also be funny. Norman admitted to himself that she grew on a guy. Also, he had to admit that Lily was never boring.

So, with his nose buried in his camera book, he studied all about how to use his birthday gift with all its lens settings and attachments. When Norman was reading, no one could get his attention. So, after trying for at least three minutes to talk to Norman, Lily left him alone and went off to find someone else to listen to her.

Finally, Norman jumped up from his deep chair in the den where he had retreated from the rest of the family – especially Lily – and ran up to his room. From behind four books on his shelves he drew a wooden box that held his secret stash. All the money he earned from doing jobs for Mother around their big city house, he hid away in his special box. He took ten dollars out, pulled on his jacket, ran down the two sets of stairs to the bottom floor, and outside to the street. In the corner store, Norman bought two rolls of film for his camera, and dashed back up the street. He fairly flew up to his top floor room in the back of the house.

In no time at all, Norman had opened the back of his camera, inserted a roll of film and drawn out the end until the little holes on both edges fit the bumps inside the case, and snapped the case shut. He heard the film inside the camera turning to the first picture.

Then he was ready. He stood at a tall window where he could see far down the back lane behind the house. He flicked the little button that zoomed the lens, and held the camera up to his eye to look through the tiny view window. Slowly he turned the distance settings on the front of the camera to get the clearest picture – and quickly took the camera away from his eye. Again he raised the camera to his right eye. No. There it was again. He did not see the lane below as he had expected. What Norman saw, looking right back into his brown eye, was a piercing, blue eye.

Now, Norman was a boy who saw things pretty much the way they really were. While Lily sometimes dreamed up the most fantastic stories about her adventures, Norman was a clear thinker. Of course, there was that one time in the park when he had taken a swim in the lake and almost drowned in a storm. He could still remember clearly that he had been saved – carried gently to the shore by a tall Being who must have been an angel, for its great white feathered wings had swept the towering waves aside. The angel's eyes were blue and flashed like brilliant stones.

No one knew about his angel, not Dad or Mother and especially not Lily. Of course, Lily had told him her secret about climbing to the top of the castle keep on the island

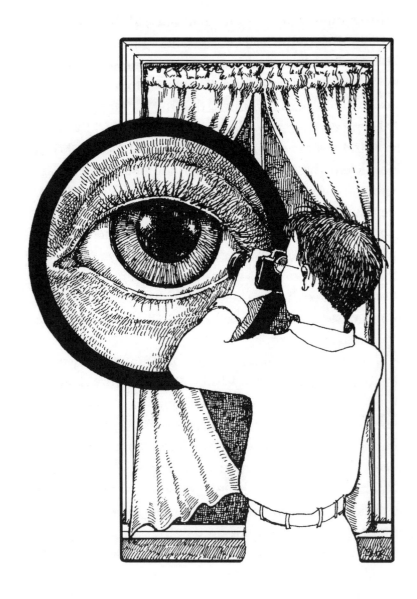

*What Norman saw was a piercing blue eye*

and seeing her angel. But then, Lily never could keep a secret. And he was glad, because hearing about her angel made his angel seem more real to him. He had been tempted to think that none of it had ever happened.

Very carefully, Norman lifted his camera again and put his eye to the little window. Maybe he had seen a blue eye, and maybe he did not see any such thing. This time, he was relieved to see a clear view of the street at the far end of the lane. He could even see his friend Jake riding his bike and turning the corner down the lane. His camera lens was like a telescope, and Norman could clearly see the dark spot on Jake's cheek where he had bumped into a door in the fence behind his house. He was having so much fun playing with his camera that he did not hear his mother calling.

'Norman,' Mother called from the bottom of the stairs. 'Supper! Please come down.'

Lily met Norman in the hall, and they raced down the two flights of stairs. Lily's short legs could not keep up with Norman, though, and by the time she reached the supper table, they were all waiting for her.

'One more week until school ends for summer vacation, Kids,' said Dad. 'How would you like to go out West? We've never been there before.'

'Great! I can take my new camera.' That was just about as excited as Norman had ever talked. In fact, Lily looked at him as if she were seeing him for the first time.

'How about Arizona?' Dad suggested.

'With cowboys and Indians?' Lily was bouncing in her chair, and her voice was rising to a squeak.

'They don't have real cowboys and Indians anymore, do they, Dad?' Norman had a whole bookshelf full of books about the American West.

'We'll just have to find out.' Dad liked to tease, and sometimes Lily and Norman were not sure if he was serious. He had actually told them once that he did not have to eat spinach because it had too much iron, and the doctor had told him he would get rusty. Naturally Norman and Lily were supposed to eat their spinach, but they could not think of any reason not to eat it that Mother would accept.

Anyway, not long after that, they packed their bags, drove to the airport, and flew to the city of Phoenix in Arizona. Lily and Norman had flown before, so for four hours sitting next to each other on the plane, they mostly dozed. When they flew to England the year before, Lily had spent the time fidgeting, but she would soon be ten years old. She imagined that ten-year-old girls never fidgeted. However, when she looked out the window to the ground far below, and saw bushy desert and pointy hills which grew into craggy mountains, she forgot about being almost ten.

'Normy, it's all rocky and red and there are no houses,' she said as she poked him with her elbow.

Norman had to lean way over Lily to look out. He had to stretch so far that his nose was almost touching the window, and as he did, a flash of deep blue peered back at him from outside the plane. It was gone in a blink, but Norman had just enough time to see a pair of striped wings whirr and flit away. He looked at Lily out of the side of his right eye, to see if she had seen what he saw. But she was busy talking and munching peanuts. So he sank back into his seat, deep into his thoughts.

'Please raise your seat backs and tray tables to their fixed and upright position in preparation for landing at Phoenix airport,' announced the pilot. Norman had no time to think through what he had seen, but he tucked it all away in his mind for later.

After that, there was a rush of gathering up all their stuff, waiting to get off the plane, walking through the crowds in the terminal, collecting their luggage, and loading it all into the big car that Dad had rented. The first thing they noticed when the doors of the airport terminal opened was a sweep of heat that hit them all in the face like a blanket. Norman shed his sweater, and Lily was soon wiping sweaty drops from her rosy face.

'All right, Lily?' Mother wanted to know. She was looking over her shoulder from the front seat of the car. Lily was sitting extra carefully in the back seat, trying not to move.

'I guess so,' Lily answered in a tiny voice. She had never been so hot in her whole life.

But Norman sat cool and quiet in his corner in the back seat. He was thinking, really thinking. His camera was slung over his shoulder on its red strap, and he cradled it carefully in one hand.

Soon the car's air conditioning made them all comfy, and they began to pay attention to the city streets that soon widened into boulevards and then narrowed past stretches of desert full of low bushes and funny-looking, tall green posts with loopy green arms.

'There you are, Kids – saguaro cactus. Some of them are very old and grow to more than twenty feet tall. You never saw anything like that growing back East.' Dad would have explained more, but Norman offered that he had seen pictures of the big cactus in his books about the West. Of course, he had never heard anyone say that word out loud, until Dad pronounced it *sa-war-o*.

Dad drove for a long time in the direction of the northern mountains, while Mother read a map and directed him where to turn to get to their hotel. Off to the west, wisps of white clouds striped the sky and began to turn gold and red. Meanwhile, the sun was like a gold fire ball as it dropped slowly towards the mountain tops.

When they finally turned up a steep road that wound around high rocks and stumpy bushes, even Norman sat closer to his window. He did not want to miss anything. But when the car turned up an even steeper road and stopped, Norman was not ready for the hotel. The building was spread across and up the side of a mountain and was the same colour as the red rocks that piled up in clumps wherever they looked. None of them had even seen the building up on the mountain when they were driving hundreds of feet below on the road. The hotel just seemed to grow out of the mountain like a pile of boulders.

Norman took his camera from its case, jumped out of the car and walked back and forth on the sandy road to get the best angle for a picture of the valley down below. And when he zoomed the lens and put his eye to the window, he saw, perched on one arm of a tall prickly saguaro cactus growing just below him, a large bird. Its brown and gold striped feathers shone in the sun and its powerful wings looped out as it lifted from its perch. Norman had only a second to snap a picture, and when he looked up, the bird glided steeply toward him, turned in the air not far from Norman's camera, and blinked one deep blue eye. Then the kite soared off, climbing straight up, far above the mountain top.

'So that's it.' Norman said to himself. He was standing like a statue, hoping the bird would fly his way again.

'She's a beauty!' said a deep voice behind him.

Norman jumped and wheeled around, his camera swinging from his neck. Standing there was a tall cowboy – at least he looked like the cowboys in his books – plaid shirt, jeans, leather boots and wide-brimmed hat.

'She's a kite, a kind of hawk,' he explained. 'Haven't seen this one around here before today. Your folks are inside. Sent me out to find you.'

Norman and his guide tramped up to the hotel door and walked into a cool, wide, long room. The floor was paved with large square shiny tiles, painted with dark red and gold designs, and on one long wall was a fireplace that Norman could have walked into, standing straight up. Big, puffy chairs stood here and there, and flaming lamps hung on the walls.

Up in his room, Norman's bag had been opened, and all his clothes were hanging in a closet, with his hiking

nding beneath. He hoped he could hike in the
...s, or even ride a horse and take rolls and rolls
of film. He had just put a new roll into the back of his
camera when Lily knocked at his door.

'Supper, Nor-man,' she sang.

Just as they left the room, Norman looked back to the
window and was sure he saw a flutter of brown and gold
wings outside. He rushed to see if it was his kite, but by
the time he reached the window, there was nothing there.
'I guess I won't tell Lily about the kite' he thought. 'Not
yet, anyway.'

That night after supper, Norman and Dad took a walk
to the stables in back of the hotel. The night was cool
and quiet after the heat of the day. Now and then, as
they passed one of the short desert bushes, Norman
heard tiny rustles like something shuffling hairy legs in
dried leaves. Then he would walk closer to Dad and
move his feet just a little faster. Of course, Norman was
not afraid of things he could not see – usually.

In the dusky evening, the blazing sun sank behind the
far mountains as if it were in a hurry. Norman wondered
just what was out there. 'Out there' was a steep hillside,
covered with bushes that had white balls of pointy spines
which shone pale in the shadows.

When they finally reached the stables, they heard the
horses shuffling their feet and breathing softly in their
stalls.

'Let's choose our horses for tomorrow's ride in the
desert,' Dad suggested. They were standing in the centre
of the barn with a row of stalls on each side. Lanterns

flickered shadows all around them as they walked slowly past the sleepy horses. One or two came to the opening above the stall doors and leaned their long faces out to see who was there. Norman wanted to see into the stalls, but the doors were too high, so he had to reach up to the top of a door with both hands and pull himself up to see over the top. Dad would have helped him, but Norman liked to do things for himself.

So when he was hanging from the last stall door at the end of the row, he found himself eye to eye with the long white face of a tall horse. Norman could not move. The horse did not move. Norman felt as if some strong hand held him close to the wooden door. He was frozen. He could not take his eyes away from the bright, unblinking eyes that stared back straight into his. When Norman felt he could not hold on one more minute, he began to let go and drop to the ground. But just before he did, he saw one large flashing eye wink at him from the horse's white face.

'No,' thought Norman, 'I must have imagined that.' He let his hands go limp and slid to the ground, hearing, as he touched down, a low, soft chuckle from the other side of the stall door.

'Have you picked a horse, Norman?' Dad called from the other end of the stalls.

'Yes, this white one,' was the quiet answer.

He was tired when he got into bed that night. He usually fell into a deep sleep as soon as his head touched his pillow. But that night was different, and he slept in little naps. The next day took forever to get there.

*Yes, this white one*

In the morning, finally, at eight o'clock, right after breakfast, Norman ran to the stables. He was all ready – his new cowboy hat firmly on his head and his camera hanging around his neck over a new plaid shirt. He reached the stables just as his cowboy friend was walking the tall white horse out of the stables.

'We call him Angel,' said Joe as he helped Norman up high into the saddle. 'You picked a good one. He'll take good care of you. Just remember, when you want him to turn right, you lay the reins on the right side of his neck. And when you want him to turn left, lay them on the left side. When you're ready, just give his sides a little nudge with your heels, and he'll start to walk. OK! Everybody here?'

Joe and Dad soon swung up into their saddles, and the three of them walked their horses slowly to the beginning of a narrow trail.

Norman's heart was pumping much faster than it usually did, and yet he was not afraid – no, he was not afraid. He was last in line on the trail, and he was really glad. He was thinking that the reason he was not afraid, even though he had ridden a horse only twice before, was Angel. The big white horse even turned his head once and looked at Norman. It was a quick look, but Norman had the feeling that Angel was looking at him as if he knew him. Were the corners of the wide mouth turned up, smiling at him? No, thought Norman. No way.

'How are you doing back there, Norm?' called Joe from the front of the line. Dad turned to look back and waved.

So, for an hour, they walked their horses through the brown-red desert while they talked to each other in low voices. Then they stopped in a grove of tall cottonwood trees and sat in the shade eating sandwiches that Joe fished out of his leather saddle bag. They were just sandwiches, but to Norman they were a feast. While they ate, Joe told them stories about the Indians who lived near by. Once he looked up and pointed to a small wisp of cloud in the shape of a giant bird. But what was really strange was that the cloud was streaked with an up-and-down rainbow of colours.

'It's called a sundog,' Joe explained. While they were all looking up, a sound like crackling beans came from behind a prickly bush.

'Is it a snake, Joe?' Norman wanted to see a snake, but also he did *not* want to see a snake.

'Maybe.' Joe got up and walked to his horse. 'Let's ride on. We're not too far from the castle,' he said, as he swung his long legs over his horse. And soon they were all up in their saddles, walking their horses in the direction of the distant mountain.

'Joe! What castle?' Norman had been pretty quiet on their long ride. He had to think while he rode so that he would not fall off his horse. But by the time they left the trees, he felt safe and comfortable sitting in Angel's saddle. So when Joe said 'castle', little blond hairs stood up on the back of his neck and tickled under his shirt collar.

'Montezuma's Castle. About eight hundred years ago, some people built a kind of apartment house right into the side of a high cliff that's about seventy feet high. They found a big cave half way up, and made walls and rooms out of clay, and they lived there.'

'But Joe, how did they get up there?' Norman could feel his heart beat faster and faster. 'Can we go there? Please, Dad, can we?'

'You're sure you're not too tired?'

'No, Dad, I feel great!'

So, on they rode, and the red mountain with its hanging cliffs grew closer and closer. If Norman looked really hard, he could just see high, flat red-brown walls that seemed to grow out of the cliff. The closer they got, the faster Norman's big, powerful horse walked, until Angel finally broke into a smooth, cruising gallop. Norman crunched down over Angel's neck, his knees squeezed tightly against the horse's sides, and gave himself up to their flight across the desert. He did not know when he first realised that he was riding alone.

They were going fast, and the mountain in front of them grew so big that Norman could not see the top. In fact, he had a hard time seeing anything because the wind was whipping around him, flinging his hair into his eyes and stinging his face. Tears collected in the little creases around his eyes as he closed them to narrow slits.

Still Angel raced on – and suddenly slowed to a stroll and then stopped. The big horse lowered his head, munched a nearby bush, and then turned to look at Norman. 'Still there?' he seemed to say. As for Norman, he had been holding on so tightly to his horse that he was weak and slid to the ground with a soft thump.

*High, flat, red-brown walls seemed to grow out of the cliff*

He wrapped the reins around a tree branch in the way Joe had told him, put his hand up to shade his eyes, and looked in every direction.

No one. As far as he could see – no Joe, and no Dad.

It sank into his head that he had no idea which direction the hotel was. And just when he began to feel a large lump somewhere in his middle begin to crawl up to his throat, he remembered what Joe had said. Angel would take care of him.

No sooner had he begun to feel relieved, when Angel tugged at the reins. Norman grabbed them just in time and hung on to them, while Angel pulled his head away. So what was Norman to do? He put one foot into a stirrup and hauled himself up with all his strength.

For a few seconds, he sat in the saddle carefully and waited. Angel stood like a statue. When Norman touched the right side of the horse's neck with the reins and nudged his heels into the wide white sides, nothing happened. Norman tried again – and then again. But the horse would not move.

Once more, Norman shaded his eyes, looked at the giant mountain in front him, and knew at that moment that what he saw was the castle of Montezuma. The cliff towered high above him, and at the bottom of the mountain was a narrow trickle of a creek.

Norman was thinking so hard that he was surprised when Angel began walking softly toward the base of the mountain. In a few minutes they reached the creek, and Angel stopped, lowered his head to the cool water and buried his soft muzzle in the rippling stream.

Angel waited until Norman got out of the saddle. Beyond the creek, a rocky slope rose to a narrow ledge, and standing on the front edge reaching up to another ledge above it was a rough wooden ladder. Norman leaned his head back as far as he could and looked up to where the next ledge hung out over the valley floor, and on this ledge was another ladder leading up to the next level. He wished he could see higher, and he could not decide what to do. But at that moment, Angel pushed his nose into Norman's back, making him jump two steps toward the rising slope. Norman looked back to see his horse shake his head three times and hear him give a long, low whistle.

So Norman turned back to the mountain and began walking. At first he was careful not to walk close to the prickly balls that clung to short bushes, but soon he was walking with his eyes on the ladder above the first ledge. The ground grew steeper and rockier, until he was pulling himself up from one large rock to another one above. When he reached the first ledge, he hung on to it until he could get a leg over the top.

But he almost lost his grip when a brown and gold striped face with a pointed beak peered at him over the edge, staring with bright blue eyes right into Norman's brown eyes. The kite flipped out his wide wings to their longest length, rolled them back again close to its body, and walked back and forth on the ledge like a general taking command.

Norman was relieved to finally drag himself up on to the ledge. He wanted to get a photo of the great bird, but just as he got his camera all focused, the kite lifted off the ledge and sailed up to the ledge above him, as if waiting for him. So naturally, Norman put his camera in its case, planted one foot on the next ladder, and then holding on with all his might, he climbed up, one rung, two rungs, all the way up to the twentieth rung, and then crawled carefully onto the higher ledge.

He turned around to look behind him to the desert far below. Actually he was hoping he would see his Dad and Joe, but there was no one down there, and the sun was standing directly above him in the cloudless sky, hot and glaring.

All of the desert with the tall mountains on every side and the blue sky above would make a perfect picture. Norman swung his camera to his eye, turned the dial on the lens for just the right view, and snapped the photo. He took six or seven pictures after that, from every angle, and he was so busy that he did not at first hear the whirring sound not far from his right foot. When he did, he looked down quickly, his camera frozen to his face.

There he stood, a ball of fear rising so fast in his throat that drops of sweat rolled down between his eyes. All he could think of was his science teacher that year who had said, in a booming voice, 'A full-grown diamondback rattlesnake can kill nine men in a row.' The snake was coiled near his feet, shaking its rattled tail to a whiz.

Norman began to think about lowering his arms verrr-y slowly. Just when he thought his knees would collapse, a brown and gold striped blur dropped from the air like a stone – right to the hissing head raised near Norman's knee. Bird and snake twisted in a whirl, and then with one smooth move, the kite, gripping the snake just behind its head, flew like a shot up into the air and opened its beak. The length of snake fell far down to the desert floor like a long limp rope.

Speaking of limp – Norman's knees gave out, and he sat down in a hurry. While he sat in a heap on the rocky ledge, it occurred to him that the kite seemed bigger than when he first saw him. 'This heat is playing tricks with my head,' thought Norman.

But finally, he felt stronger, so he decided that he had to see the very top. Taking three deep breaths, he reached up to the next ladder leaning high up to the level above. This time, he climbed more slowly and tried to notice every rock. Once, he had to stop and wrap his arms around the ladder. He leaned against the rungs and tried not to look down while he got his breath.

When he reached the top of that ledge, he looked very carefully from one side to the other. A mud clay wall reached to one side of a small opening and on the other side, stretched to where the straight red brick wall ended at the far cliff edge. Standing on the ledge, Norman began to feel that someone or something was standing near, on the other side of the wall. Even so, he was not afraid.

At eye level when Norman stood on his toes, was a square hole cut into the wall. This hole was just big enough for Norman's head, so very carefully, he poked his head into the hole. At first, what he saw was a long

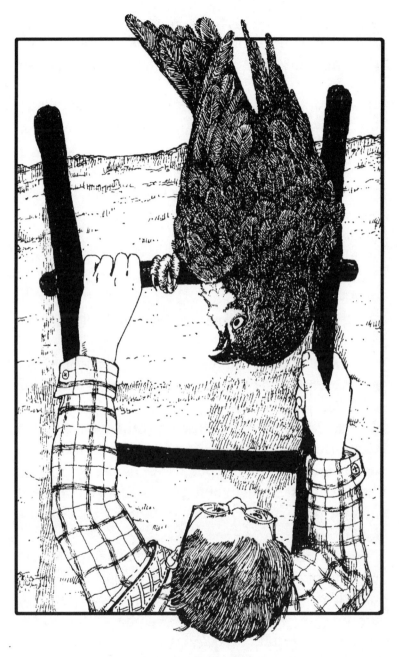

'I'm coming,' called Norman, and climbed higher

room, but he pulled his head out fast, bumping the top with a sharp whap. He had one second to hear a chirp before the kite's head burst through the hole to his side of the wall.

Limp, Norman fell down to the stone ledge, which seemed to amuse the bird, because it perched on the edge of the hole and gave him a whole string of chuckly chirps.

'Are you laughing at me?' Norman did not think it was funny at all. By now, he had bruises from his shoulders to his knees, and he could feel them growing purple.

'Chirp-ity.'

'You *are* laughing at me.'

'Chiroop. Chiroop.'

'OK, I'm going. Two more ladders and I'll be at the top.'

'Chiray. Chiray.' With that, the great bird looped out his wings, lifted off his perch, and flew up beyond to the next ledge. Norman stood up in spite of his aching knees and was soon climbing slowly up the next wooden ladder. This time, he thought he would never make it to the top, but when he stopped to rest on the tenth rung, half way up, the brown and gold kite looked down at him from the ledge overhead and chirped a whole string of whistles.

'I'm coming,' called Norman and climbed higher and higher until he finally stepped onto the last ledge. This time when he turned to look down at the desert, he could hardly see the bushes or the creek at the bottom of the cliff. Also, he could not see Angel.

But he had no time to worry about that. The sun was almost gone behind the far mountains. A chilly wind began to lift his light hair, and he shivered once. So he was relieved when he saw near his left shoulder, a short doorway in the mud wall. It was so short that even he had to duck so he would not bump the top. Bowing his head, Norman stepped through.

In the long room, seven lamps hung on the back rock wall, flickering shadows at his feet. When his eyes got used to the glowing room, Norman saw that the long wall was covered with pictures – wings spread wide – hands with long fingers, that lifted up to point to golden stars – and in the centre of the stars above the centre lamp, a lamb whose white fleece shone brighter than all the lamps together. So brightly did the lamb shine that Norman put his hand to his eyes the way he had shielded them from the afternoon sun.

Norman sat down with legs crossed on the smooth clay floor, never taking his eyes from the lamb glowing above, and as he did, a strong, low voice from the shadowy corner spoke. Each word was like a musical note, but he had never heard such music before. It drifted down on his head, smooth and light, touching his hair like the brush of a feather.

'My child. You did well to climb all the way up. Now you know that you need never doubt that I will keep you safe, and never be afraid.'

'Are you my angel from the park?' Norman looked into the shadows, but the long room was dark except for the white lamb shining like the brightest star.

'I told you I would see you again, Norman.'

With these words, Norman felt strong arms lift him up until he stood on his feet. Then huge brown-gold wings swept beneath him and whisked him through the low door. He wrapped his arms around the feathered neck and hung on the way he had clung to Angel when they galloped across the desert. Norman and his kite flew beyond the high ledge, up through the night sky, far out and up to the top of the mountain, his hair streaming in the cool air.

When they reached the highest craggy point, the kite stood, looked over his shoulder, turned a flashing blue eye on Norman, swept the darkness three times with his great wings, and then plunged toward the earth. One second more, and the kite settled feather-light to the desert floor.

Norman found he was standing near something large that glowed whitely in the starlight. A soft whinny told him that Angel was waiting for him to climb up into his saddle. As he did, brown-gold wings brushed his face and floated off to the stars.

'Norman!' came the call in the darkness, 'We've been looking everywhere for you. Joe and his friends from the hotel have been riding around here for hours.'

Dad was so glad to see Norman, he leapt off his horse and ran to his son who was sitting tall and strong in Angel's saddle. It was Norman, all right, but a different Norman. Flaming around them was a ring of torches where Joe and the other cowboys waited, the flickering lights shining in Norman's eyes, turning them to gold.

*Beyond the high ledge, up through the night sky*

All the way back to the hotel, Norman tried to tell Dad and Joe about climbing up to Montezuma's Castle. But hard as he tried, it was impossible to make them understand. He decided that it was one of those you-had-to-be-there days. At least he had his photographs – but his pictures would not help him explain the best part. One day it would all be clear – to them and to him, too.

THE END

# The Castle King

'Normy?'

'Lily, please!'

'Oh. I'm really sorry, Normy. I'll start again.' Lily counted to ten while Norman sighed a small sigh.

'Norman?'

'Yes, Lily.'

'Are there castles everywhere in the world?' Lily thought about castles almost every day.

She and Norman were sitting on the warm white sand while the tail ends of waves floated between their toes. They were resting after a long morning of carrying buckets of wet sand from the ocean edge, up the beach to where they had built a sand castle. It had walls as high as Lily's waist and turrets and towers above the walls, some higher than the others. Some towers were round and some were square. After they had built all the towers, they cut out square openings two inches apart all around the top of each wall with the sharp end of a small shovel. Then they cut out little windows around and up and down the towers. They agreed that it looked exactly like the castle they had visited in England the year before.

Way out in the ocean, the waves built up to tall roaring towers of water and then broke with pounding crashes and rolled smoothly up the beach.

One time, when Lily was seven years old, she had stood in the shallows waving to Mother and Dad who were sitting far up on the sand. Her back was to the ocean, and she had not seen a big roller of a wave tearing towards her. It had broken over her, turning her upside down, pushing her this way and that, side to side in a tumble. Underneath the swirling water, Lily bounced against shells and pebbles, scraping her knees and losing her breath.

At the very second when she thought she would never reach the top, no matter how hard she struggled, the water had pushed her up and her head had popped out of the moving wave. Lily was gasping and choking, and she had sat still in the shallow water as the wave swung back out to sea.

When her heart had stopped pounding, Lily had stood up with a loud huff and limped carefully up the beach to where her towel was spread on the sand near Mother. She could hardly talk as she flopped down onto her towel and fell asleep in the hot sun. When it was time to leave, Norman had shaken her for two minutes before she could wake up.

Every summer, Dad and Mother rented a cottage at the seashore for a week. They would have to pack up their clothes and blankets and sheets and all their stuff, load it into their car in the city, and drive for two hours to Ocean City on the Atlantic Ocean. After a week of playing in the sand and riding the waves, Norman would be tanned a golden brown, and Lily would be red and peely. Strips of dried white skin would begin to flake and pull from her arms. So Lily and her friend Gail would sit on their big beach towels and peel each other's shoulders, making a little pile of skin peels heaped on the towel.

'Lily! That's disgusting!' Norman would say.

But Lily thought it was fun – until the day she got so burned sleeping on the beach that her knees were painful and she could not bend them.

Meanwhile, Norman and his friends were always busy on the beach – at least until one week, when a pretty yellow-haired girl arrived from the city. Norman had stopped spending so much time with the guys, and began to sit on the beach talking for hours to Heather.

'Normy's got a gur-rel friend!' Lily sang. And she would not stop.

So, of course, Norman chased Lily down the beach into the water. But she still sang, 'Gur-rel friend! Gur-rel friend!' and Norman ducked her under the water. When she came up sputtering, she could not sing anything.

'You never did know when to stop, Lily.' Norman just tramped off without another word.

But as I was saying, one day Norman and Lily were sitting on the beach with their feet in the shallow water, resting from a whole morning of building their castle.

'Don't know, Lily. Maybe there are castles all over the world. We saw the castle in the park near home. And there was the one in England when we lived there for a year. And there was the one in Arizona. You didn't see that one up close, but I did.

'Norman, are you ever going to tell me what happened to you at Mazuma's Castle?'

'Montezuma's Castle, Lily. Anyway, you didn't tell me all about what happened to you when we were at the Castle in England – at least not much.'

'It was sooooo– I met the most wonderful knight and he– he– I just don't know how to tell you, Normy.' Usually, Lily had whole paragraphs of things to say – more than enough for a ten-year-old girl.

'I know. I can't explain my castle either, or my kite – he led me up to the top of the castle on the mountain. He had blue eyes that flashed when he looked at me.

'Normy! I mean, Norman! Me, too – my knight's eyes were blue just like that – all lit up and blue. And my angel in the Castle Keep – he had the same blue eyes.'

'My angel did, too, the one in the park,' Norman said in a low voice.

'What do you think it means, Norman?'

The two of them sat and thought so long and hard that they never realised when the ocean's tide sent waves higher and higher on the sand. When they found that not only their toes were under water, but they were sitting in the shallows of incoming waves, Norman and Lily stood and walked quietly up the beach to the cottage. All the way back, neither one of them said a word.

*What do you think it means, Norman?*

One day about four months later, during Christmas vacation from school, Norman was standing at his window staring at the cold, grey sky. He was feeling quiet, and he could not stop thinking about castles and angels. So he reached for his photograph album. He opened it to the pictures of Arizona that he had snapped with the camera he got for his thirteenth birthday.

He sat staring at the photos, especially six pictures of his brown and gold striped kite with its brilliant blue eyes. The powerful bird had helped him to climb high up a huge, red mountain until they reached Montezuma's castle on a cliff hanging above the desert. He wished he had a picture of the wall drawings in the room at the top of the castle. He remembered how the drawing of a white lamb dazzled in the light of tall flaming lamps hanging on the walls.

'Norman?' Lily called from the doorway of her brother's room.

'What? I'm thinking.'

'I've been thinking, too. In every castle we've been to, we have never seen a king. I thought kings lived in castles.'

No sooner had Lily said the word 'king' when Norman, who was staring at a photo of his kite, saw the big bird blink a blue eye. Quickly, Norman looked away and then back at the photo. There it was again. Again and again, he looked away then back at the photo, and each time he looked at the kite's photo, the bird blinked at him. Norman must have looked funny, because Lily giggled and said, 'Normy, what are you doing? Your head is jumping back and forth.'

'Lily, come here. You want to see something?' Norman tugged Lily's arm until she was standing next to the photo album on Norman's desk. 'Look at this picture of the kite, and tell me what you see.'

Lily stood quietly and looked hard at the picture – and nearly jumped out of her skin. 'He smiled at me! He did! The bird smiled.'

'But Lily, he blinked at me! Are you sure?'

The two of them spent a long time taking turns looking at the kite's photo. And each time Lily looked, she saw the bird smile at her, but when Norman looked, the kite blinked an eye. Finally, Norman closed the album.

'One more time, Norman!' Lily pleaded.

'Do you know what I think? I think we should go back to the park and see if we can find the castle keep again.' Norman's voice sounded very serious, as if he were in church. 'Maybe this time we will see the king.'

'Right! We've got to go back to the castle keep,' agreed Lily.

That night, Norman could not get to sleep for a long time. In the first place, his sheets would not lie still. Just when he got all settled in his bed with his sheet pulled up to his chin, the sheet would flutter up in the air with a whoosh and settle back down, covering his face. This went on for quite a while, until Norman, holding down his sheet with both fists, closed his eyes, in spite of the silly sheet, and fell into a light sleep. But it seemed to Norman that he was wakened every hour by the sound of beating wings that tickled his ears. Each time, he would have to tackle his sheet to make it stop whooshing.

Meanwhile in her room, Lily was trying to keep her pillow from sliding off the bed onto the floor. Every time she had her head in the exact middle of her pillow, it slipped off the edge of her bed like melted butter. Finally,

after getting out of bed and picking her pillow up for the seventh time, she punched her pillow with both fists and then hung on to it tightly until she fell asleep. But all night long she dreamed she was riding a tall white horse down endless paths between tall hedges, trying to find her way out of a maze, knowing she was completely lost.

The next morning, Lily could hardly wait to tell Norman about her sliding pillow, but he was waiting to tell her about his frisky sheet.

'That does it! We're going to the park – today!' Norman had never sounded so serious, and Lily looked at him carefully. It seemed to her that her brother was becoming a different person, and she did not always understand him.

After breakfast, Lily went up to her room to put on her hiking shoes. And when she dashed down the steps to the bottom floor, Norman was waiting for her. They both wore heavy coats with long wool scarves wrapped around their necks, and hats and gloves. Lily's red hat almost matched her fat, red curls. They left quickly and walked very fast through the streets.

They were in a hurry, but also, the cold, grey sky looked like snow. Norman was still taller than Lily, so she had to remind him at least five times, 'Normy, wait up.' Her short legs could never keep up with him.

In twenty minutes, Norman and Lily reached their grassy park and found the little stone bridge where they had crossed over to the island almost two years before. On the other side of the bridge, they stood and wondered which way to go. There was only one path, but it stretched through the trees in both directions. Norman pointed to the right, and they walked quickly into the woods.

The last time they had walked through the woods on this island, the bushes were loaded with flowers, red, orange and yellow, that crowded the rocky path. And the trees had been so leafy that the sun could not reach down to the path, so that Lily had become lost in the woods. But this time, the tall trees were bare brown limbs, and only a few bushes were still a dusty green.

At first, Lily and Norman walked past the brown trees without talking. Then, because it seemed as if they were walking for a long time, Norman began to tell Lily about his climb up to the cliff castle high above the desert in Arizona. When he got to the part about how his kite swooped down on a rattlesnake coiled next to Norman's leg and how the kite flung the snake off the cliff, Lily froze. 'Oh, Normy, how awful. What did you do?'

'I kept climbing. Come on, Lily. We need to keep going.'

What really stopped Lily in the middle of the path was when Norman described the room at the top of the castle, all about the wall pictures, the shining lamb in a ring of stars.

'I heard a strong voice that told me not to doubt he would care for me and not to be afraid. And then, the kite seemed to grow bigger. He flew under me, and I hung on to him while he flew me to the top of the mountain, and then we flew down to the desert. The kite had bright blue eyes.'

'But that's just like my knight.' Lily was getting so excited she could not stand still and she could not walk on. ' 'Member when we all went to the castle in England when Daddy was working in London, and Crystal and Beau went with us, and—'

'I remember all that, Lily. What happened?' Norman could not wait for Lily to get to the point.

'I'm telling you. I went to a great hall in the castle while the rest of you went outside. My knight was there, and he was all covered in shiny armour, and even his horse had armour on his sides and on his head. So while I was looking at him, his helmet opened, and he looked at me and winked. And then I ran outside to the opening in the hedge maze, and I went into the maze first. And I walked and walked and I finally got to the centre, and guess what! My knight was there! And he told me all about his special armour, and guess what!

'You don't have to say "guess what" each time, Lily.'

'Right! Anyway, he told me to kneel, and he lifted up his sword and laid it on my shoulders one at a time, and named me Child of Truth.' Lily's voice had turned soft as if she were singing her favourite song.

Lily and Norman walked and talked and tried to work out what it all meant. They were thinking so hard about their mystery, that Norman jumped almost straight up in the air when Lily grabbed his arm and shouted, 'Normy! What's that?'

'Lily. Don't ever do that again!'

'But Normy, look!'

'Where?'

What Norman saw when Lily pointed to the woods, was a tall, dark grey shadow standing between thin brown trees. Lily hung on to Norman's arm, and they walked faster. Around a little bend in the path, Norman saw another grey shadow, even taller.

He hurried Lily along faster. But no matter how fast they walked, the two grey shadows, one on each side of the path in the trees, seemed to keep up with them. Finally, Norman and Lily were almost running, and the shadows floated between the trees just as fast as they ran. But what was worse, every time they looked, there seemed to be more tall shadows, slipping easily between the winter trees – ahead of them, behind them, all around them.

They had no idea how far they ran. At last, Lily almost choked, 'Norman, I'm so tired,' as she hurried along the path, hanging on to Norman's hand as hard as she could.

'We've been in the woods for an hour,' panted Norman. They were so deep in the trees he was not sure which direction they were going. And there was no castle. Nothing but trees.

'Norman! What's that over there? I think I see grey stones.' Lily began to run faster between crackling bushes, hearing as she ran a small song that swirled around her ears like wind. Right away, Lily knew the song. It was the same one she had heard before at the castle keep.

'Do you hear it, Normy?' Lily puffed between breaths.

But Norman was running fast behind her, and he did not hear her. And he did not hear the music, because in the trees not far ahead, he saw the flash of striped brown and gold wings spread wide and sweeping the air. Norman was thinking, 'I'm not surprised. I should have known.' But out loud he called to the kite, 'Wait! Wait for me!'

Norman and Lily ran so fast they crashed through the close bushes and stopped suddenly, almost thumping into each other. In front of them was a small stone house in a ring of tall trees. Pale smoke wisped from the chimney, and looking up, Norman and Lily saw white snowy flakes floating down to them, shining brightly in the woodland clearing.

'I have been waiting for you, Norman and Lily.'

Stepping through the trees was a person they had never seen before. He was dressed in a long grey coat with a blue wool scarf wound around his neck, and his hair shone like gold.

'How do you know our names?' asked Norman.

'I have to know your names. I work for the master of the castle.'

'But we've been looking for the castle keep in the woods. We saw it before, Sir,' Lily said softly.

'There is no castle keep in these woods.'

'But I climbed up to the top of the tower, and I saw an angel,' Lily explained.

'And I swam in the lake and an angel rescued me,' added Norman. 'Do you live in this house? Who is the master?'

'The master is the Great King.' With these words, the lightly falling snow began to sparkle like diamonds and settle on Lily and Norman like separate little stars until their eyelashes flashed in the dim woods.

'We've been looking for the king. We want to see him, Sir,' said Norman.

'The Great King does live in a castle – a heavenly castle.'

'But how can we see him?' Norman and Lily were beginning to think they would never find the king.

'The Great King cannot welcome anyone to his castle who does not love him. You can understand that, can't you?'

Before either Lily or Norman could answer, he explained. 'Here is the mystery. The Great King has always loved you, even though you have not always loved him. In fact, sometimes you act as if you hate him.'

'I'm sorry, Sir,' whispered Lily.

'But what do we have to do to live with the Great King in his castle?' Norman looked at Lily, and saw that she might cry. 'Please, Sir, what can we do?'

'Nothing. There is nothing you can do.' When Lily heard that, she felt one tear begin to slide down her cheek where it froze to crystal in the cold air.

'Don't cry, dear Lily. The King's son has already done all that can be done.' Sir's voice began to sound like the beautiful music Lily remembered. When she looked up to his face, she saw that his eyes were the same as the deep blue eyes of her angel.

'The Great King's son will take you to his castle.' The blue eyes began to flash. 'He left his father's castle many years ago to live down here on earth. He agreed to be punished in your place for your disobedience.' Flashes of blue light shot through the falling snow, lighting up the circling trees and Lily's teary face.

'Men killed the son of the Great King because they hated him, even though he was perfectly innocent. And he allowed them to kill him.'

'Like killing a lamb?' Norman asked.

'Yes, just like an innocent lamb.'

'Now I understand,' thought Norman, 'the lamb on the castle wall.'

'He did this for me?' Lily brushed hot tears from her cheeks.

'Yes. But soon afterward, the son burst out of his tomb. Death could not hold him, and he went home to the Great King.'

Suddenly, Sir's long grey coat fell down to the new snow. His blue scarf flew up from his neck and settled on a high tree limb. Great, powerful white wings unfolded and spread up and out, as he grew taller and taller, until his golden hair touched the top of a tree.

'"I am satisfied," said the Great King, as he welcomed his son back to his heavenly castle.' The angel's voice was deep and soft and burrowed deep down inside the listening children. 'But you must believe that the son has done all that the Great King asks. He died for you.'

The Castle King

*It's getting late. Let's go home*

Norman and Lily stood like statues in the snow that glowed gold at their feet. What Norman saw was a towering angel with the blue eyes of a powerful kite. What Lily saw was an angel that shone like glittering, silver armour.

'Please, Sir, we want to live with the Great King and his son.'

'Then you shall – if you trust and love him because he died for you, he will adopt you for his own son and daughter. But for a while, the Great King's spirit will live inside you. All through your lives, you can be a castle where the Great King will live.

'We will be his castles.'

Norman and Lily looked at each other in amazement. From where they stood, they saw the stone bridge through the trees. When they turned to thank their angel, they saw only the woods filling up with snow. What's more, the shadows were gone.

'It's getting late, Lily. Let's go home.'

Norman pulled his scarf closer to his neck and put his arm around Lily's shoulders. They walked slowly to the bridge, while a huge gold moon rose close by in the trees, lighting their faces that sparkled like new snow.

THE END